D1123340

Mrs. Gaddy and the Fast-Growing Vine

by WILSON GAGE

pictures by MARYLIN HAFNER

GREENWILLOW BOOKS · NEW YORK

Library of Congress Cataloging in Publication Data

Steele, Mary Q.
Mrs. Gaddy and the fast-growing vine.
(A Greenwillow read-alone book)
Summary: Mrs. Gaddy buys a fast-growing
vine that begins to take over her house,
her animals, and herself.
1. Children's stories, American.
[1. Humorous stories]
I. Hafner, Marylin, ill.   II. Title.
III. Series: Greenwillow read-alone books.
PZ7.S8146Mj   1985   [E]   84-18767
ISBN 0-688-04231-7
ISBN 0-688-04232-5 (lib. bdg.)

For my mother, with love
—W. G.

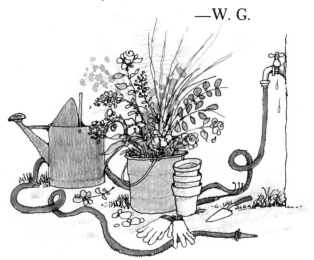

For H. B. C., vine-fighter
—M. H.

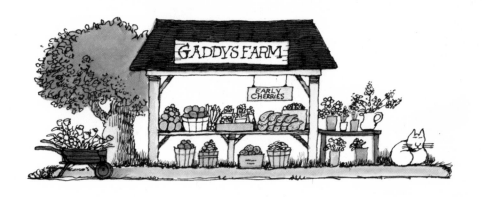

Mrs. Gaddy was a farmer.

She grew many vegetables.

She raised cherries and apples

and strawberries.

But Mrs. Gaddy loved flowers.

So she also grew roses

and lilies and snapdragons.

She grew lilacs and

black-eyed Susans.

One day Mrs. Gaddy went out

to pick some roses.

"Oh, my!" she cried.

"Everything looks so pretty.

There is just one bare spot

by the kitchen door.

I think I need a vine to grow there."

Mrs. Gaddy went to the barn.

She hitched her mule to her wagon.

She drove to town.

In the market a man

was selling plants.

"Do you have a vine for sale?"

asked Mrs. Gaddy.

"I want a vine that will grow fast.

I want a vine with pretty flowers."

"Here is just the thing,"

said the salesman. "This vine

has pretty purple flowers and

it grows as fast as lightning."

When Mrs. Gaddy got home,
she planted the new vine.
The next morning
she hurried out to look at it.
"My stars!" she cried. "Here is
a new green shoot already.
What a fast vine!"

Mrs. Gaddy went about her chores.
That afternoon she looked again.
The shoot had grown.
It was as tall as she was.
"Good!" said Mrs. Gaddy. "This vine
will soon cover that bare spot."
Next morning when she woke up,
she saw something at her window.
"Good gravy!" she yelled.
"That vine is trying
to come in my window."

11

She got her pruning shears
and went outside.
"Oh, my stars and stuffing!"
shouted Mrs. Gaddy.

The vine now had three shoots.
One was growing
in Mrs. Gaddy's bedroom window.

One was coiling around the chimney.

One was curling over the roof.

Mrs. Gaddy pruned all three shoots.

"There," she said. "That ought

to slow it down." But no.

That afternoon the vine

had four new shoots.

Mrs. Gaddy cut all the shoots
down to the ground.
But two days later the vine
had grown again.
It was bigger than ever.

"My sainted snakes!"
cried Mrs. Gaddy. "This vine
is trying to eat me alive."

She got an ax and chopped
and chopped the vine.
"That fixed it," she said.
"I will buy a rosebush
to plant in that bare spot."

But during the night
that vine started growing again.
Mrs. Gaddy tried to dig it up.
But the roots went too deep
into the ground. The vine
just went on growing.
Soon Mrs. Gaddy's house
was covered with that vine.

The leaves grew over the windows.
They shut out the light.
The stalks grew across
the kitchen door. Mrs. Gaddy
could hardly get through it.

Mrs. Gaddy was at her wits' end.
"This vine is swallowing my house,"
she said. "Soon it will swallow me
and my mule and my cow.
What shall I do?" She poured
boiling water on the vine.
But it went on growing.

She poured molasses on it.

"Molasses is so slow," she said.

"And it is sticky.

Surely molasses

will slow down this vine."

But the vine sent up

more long green shoots.

Mrs. Gaddy sprinkled it

with salt and pepper and mustard.

But the vine went on growing.

Mrs. Gaddy piled stones on the vine,

but the vine just grew around them.

She put her big soup pot over it.

But new shoots just wriggled

out from under the pot.

"Oh, tarnation!" said Mrs. Gaddy.

Suddenly she had an idea.

She hitched her mule to her wagon

and drove to town.

In the market

a man was selling goats.

"Are these goats good eaters?"

asked Mrs. Gaddy.

"These goats can eat a bulldozer,"

said the salesman.

"Then sell me the one

with the biggest appetite!"

cried Mrs. Gaddy.

23

When Mrs. Gaddy got home,

she led the goat up to the vine.

"Now eat!" she told it.

The goat ate.

It ate all the leaves.

It ate all the flowers.

It ate all the long curly stems.

Every time a new shoot sprang up,

the goat ate it.

It ate and ate.

It dug up the ground

with its sharp hooves.

It ate all the roots.

Mrs. Gaddy watched closely.

There were no more green shoots.

"Oh, what a good goat!" she cried.

"I think you have done for that vine!"

"Baaah!" said the goat

and rolled its yellow eyes.

"But bless my big toe!"

said Mrs. Gaddy. "What will

I do with this goat now?"

The goat began to eat a rosebush.

"Stop that!" yelled Mrs. Gaddy.

The goat paid no attention.

It finished the rosebush

and began to eat a lilac.

"Now you quit that!"

screamed Mrs. Gaddy.

She stamped her foot. The goat

ate a whole row of snapdragons.

"I'll chase it into the barn

with my broom," Mrs. Gaddy said.

She went to get a broom.

While Mrs. Gaddy was gone,

the goat ran around the house.

Mrs. Gaddy's front door stood open.

The goat walked in.

It ate some flowers in a vase.

It ate a lampshade.

It began to eat the rug.

Mrs. Gaddy came out
the kitchen door.
She waved her broom.
"Now where has that goat gone?"
she wondered. "I hope it has gone
a long way from here.
As long as I have my broom,
I will sweep the front steps."

Mrs. Gaddy went around her house.

She saw the open door.

She saw the goat eating her rug.

"Oh, my stars and stockings!"

she yelled.

She chased the goat out of the house.

She chased it into the barn.

The goat began to eat some hay.

"Whatever shall I do?"
cried Mrs. Gaddy.
"I can't let this awful goat
eat all the hay and oats.
How would I feed my mule?
And my cow?"

The goat ate and ate.

Mrs. Gaddy brought it

some green beans

and some potatoes

and some gingerbread.

It ate them all
and looked about for more.
"I could lock it in my storm cellar,"
said Mrs. Gaddy.
"There is nothing to eat there.
But then it would starve.
I can't let it starve."

She thought and thought.
"Maybe I could buy another vine
for it to eat," she said.
Suddenly she had an idea.
She hitched her mule
to her wagon.

She put a lot of gingerbread
in the wagon.
The goat jumped in the wagon
to eat the gingerbread.
Mrs. Gaddy jumped in too.
She drove to town.

She saw the man who had
sold the vine to her.
"Have you sold any more
of those vines?" asked Mrs. Gaddy.
"Oh, yes," said the salesman.
"Mrs. Green bought one
just this morning. She wanted
a vine to grow on her fence."

Mrs. Gaddy drove on.

She drove very fast.

The goat had eaten

all the gingerbread.

It began to eat

the wagon seat.

Very soon they came to

Mrs. Green's house.

"Oh, Mrs. Gaddy,"
said Mrs. Green.
"Look at this vine.
I have just planted it and
already it has put up a shoot."

"I have brought you a present,
Mrs. Green," said Mrs. Gaddy.
She got out of the wagon.
The goat got out of the wagon.
Mrs. Gaddy tied the goat
to the fence.

44

"That is very kind of you,
    but I really don't need a goat,"
    said Mrs. Green.
    Mrs. Gaddy looked at the vine.
    Another shoot was sprouting.
    "I think you need a goat
    very badly," she said.

She got back in her wagon
and drove away.
"I will plant a rosebush
in that bare spot,"
she said to herself.

"Roses grow slowly.

But there is no need to be

in such a hurry.

It only leads to trouble!"

WILSON GAGE is the pen name of Mary Q. Steele, who has written many popular books for children. As Wilson Gage, she is the author of two other tales about Mrs. Gaddy, *Mrs. Gaddy and the Ghost* and *The Crow and Mrs. Gaddy,* and two ALA Notable Books, *Squash Pie* and *Down in the Boondocks.* Under her own name, she is the author of *Journey Outside,* a Newbery Honor Book, as well as many other books including *Wish Come True* and *The First of the Penguins.* Born and raised in Tennessee, Ms. Steele lives there today in Chattanooga.

MARYLIN HAFNER studied at Pratt Institute and the School of Visual Arts in New York City. She does editorial illustrations for *Cricket* and other leading magazines and has illustrated many distinguished books, including *Mrs. Gaddy and the Ghost* and *The Crow and Mrs. Gaddy* by Wilson Gage, *Mind Your Manners* by Peggy Parish, *It's Halloween* by Jack Prelutsky, *Camp KeeWee's Secret Weapon* and *Jenny and the Tennis Nut* by Janet Schulman, and *Big Sisters Are Bad Witches* by Morse Hamilton. Ms. Hafner lives in Cambridge, Massachusetts.